Don't Put Yourself Down in

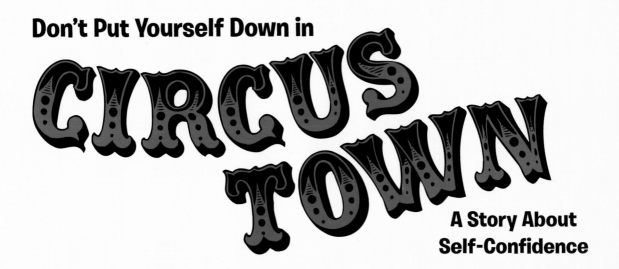

CIRCUS
TOWN

A Story About
Self-Confidence

to Ozzie and Bella. For always making our home a three-ring circus—*FJS*

for Alder Everett Ross with love—*SC*

Published by
MAGINATION PRESS
An Educational Publishing Foundation Book
American Psychological Association
750 First Street, NE
Washington, DC 20002

For more information about our books, including a complete catalog, please write to us, call 1-800-374-2721, or visit our website at www.apa.org/pubs/magination.

Printed by Phoenix Color Corporation, Hagerstown, MD
Book design by Gwen Grafft

Library of Congress Cataloging-in-Publication Data

Sileo, Frank J., 1967-
  Don't put yourself down in Circus Town : a story about self-confidence / by Frank J. Sileo, PhD ; illustrated by Sue Cornelison.
      pages cm
  "American Psychological Association."
  Summary: Ringmaster Rick calls an emergency meeting to boost the self-confidence of Circus Town's performers after hearing several put themselves down for mistakes made while rehearsing their acts. Includes note to parents.
  ISBN 978-1-4338-1913-1 (hardcover) — ISBN 1-4338-1913-9 (hardcover) — ISBN 978-1-4338-1914-8 (pbk.) — ISBN 1-4338-1914-7 (pbk.) [1. Self-confidence—Fiction. 2. Determination (Personality trait)—Fiction. 3. Circus—Fiction.] I. Cornelison, Sue, illustrator. II. Title. III. Title: Do not put yourself down in Circus Town.
  PZ7.S582Don 2014
  [E]—dc23
                          2014030923

Manufactured in the United States of America
First printing October 2014
10 9 8 7 6 5 4 3 2 1

Don't Put Yourself Down in
CIRCUS TOWN

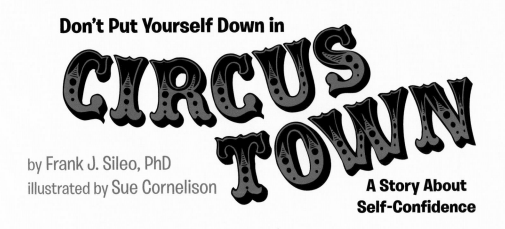

by Frank J. Sileo, PhD

illustrated by Sue Cornelison

**A Story About
Self-Confidence**

Magination Press • Washington, DC • American Psychological Association

Ringmaster Rick was excited for the
big show at Circus Town!
He visited the big tent to see all the
performers practicing their acts.

"Roarey and Clawey, I need you to jump
through this ring and then stand on two legs,"
Larry the Lion Tamer told the lions.

Roarey jumped through
the ring and rolled over instead
of standing on two legs.

Clawey got the ring
stuck on his big mane!

Larry threw up his arms.
"I am the worst lion tamer ever!"

"Wait," said Ringmaster Rick.
Larry stomped out of the ring.

Ringmaster Rick went to the other side of
the tent where Juan and Juanita, the world-
famous trapeze artists, were flying high
above. Juan was having a hard time grabbing
onto Juanita as they swung back and forth.

After several tries, Juan climbed down off the trapeze. Juan cried, "I can't do this! I am such a loser! I'm terrible at everything."

"No way," said Ringmaster Rick. Juan and Juanita left the trapeze area. They were so upset they could not hear what Ringmaster Rick said to them.

Next, Ringmaster Rick
visited Polka Dot Patti.

She was practicing juggling
several bowling pins
while riding a unicycle. As
she was practicing, she lost
her balance and went
KURPLUNK! on the ground.

Polka Dot Patti picked herself up. "I am such a klutz! All the other clowns are better than me!"

Ringmaster Rick was puzzled. "What is happening to our circus? Everyone seems to be having trouble with their self-confidence." He decided to call a meeting for everyone in Circus Town.

"I noticed that some of
you are not believing in
your skills and have been
putting yourselves down.

When you put yourself
down, it's almost like you
are bullying yourself."

Dougie the Dog Trainer looked up, surprised. "Bullying ourselves? I thought bullies are people who say and do mean things to others."

"That's correct. But when you put yourself down, you are being mean to yourself, like a bully. When you say mean things about yourself over and over, you can hurt your self-confidence," Ringmaster Rick explained. "You might want to give up or stop believing in yourself."

Ringmaster Rick told
the performers,
"Everyone makes mistakes.
No one is perfect."

"We all **bumble, stumble,
and fumble,**" yelled Terry
the Tightrope Walker.

"That's right! We all bumble, stumble, and fumble. So to build your self-confidence, you could practice more, ask for help, take deep breaths, and think helpful thoughts," Ringmaster Rick told the group.

Alex the Acrobat asked, "What are some helpful thoughts?"

"Yes! Those are all helpful thoughts," said Ringmaster Rick. "Thinking helpful thoughts will take practice. Unhelpful, put-down thoughts are like sticky cotton candy that's difficult to get unstuck."

"If you forget some of these thoughts you can always think: **Give myself a break. Anyone can make a mistake.**"

After the meeting, everyone went back to practice their acts. When Roarey and Clawey had trouble with the act, Larry said, "Let's keep practicing. We can learn from our mistakes. Let's try it again."

Juan and Juanita asked their coach for help. Their coach gave them tips to make their act better. After several successful catches, Juan told Juanita, "So glad we didn't give up." "Me too!" said Juanita.

Polka Dot Patti did
a great job with juggling,
but she did fall off
the unicycle again.

She felt embarrassed,
but she took a deep
breath and let it out
slowly. She thought,
"I don't have to be perfect.
I will work hard at
keeping my balance."

It was almost time
for the show.

"I kept practicing,
and I feel more
confident," Larry said.

Juan said, "We're
proud of ourselves.
We asked our coach
for help. Now we are
excited for our act."

"I took deep breaths and thought helpful thoughts.
I feel more positive," Polka Dot Patti said.
"I gave myself a break. Anyone can make a mistake."

The circus music began to play. Everyone backstage was getting excited. Ringmaster Rick said, "I am so proud. You are much more confident in yourselves. Now you know what to do to feel better and how to keep going when things are difficult. Let's have a great show!"

"Welcome to Circus Town!
I am Ringmaster Rick.
Let the fun and laughter begin!"

Note to Parents and Other Caregivers

As a parent or caregiver, it is very gratifying to see children display self-confidence in a variety of areas, including academics, sports, playing a musical instrument, and learning to walk, to name a few. Children who exhibit self-confidence tend to do well in school, take on new challenges, try their best, persist in activities, and have an overall more positive view of themselves.

The circus performers in this book demonstrate poor self-confidence when their acts do not go as they planned or hoped. Instead of working harder, asking for help, persevering, or engaging in positive self-talk, they give up and engage in self-defeating talk, which hinders their ability to build their self-confidence. It is not until Ringmaster Rick gives the performers advice that they are able to engage in more positive, realistic thinking, become more accepting of themselves and their abilities, and ultimately build their confidence.

What Is Self-Confidence?

Self-confidence is defined as our beliefs or thoughts about our skills and abilities. It relates to what you can actually accomplish, and what you believe or think you can do or accomplish. Examples of self-confident thoughts include, "I am good at reading," "I can make friends easily," or "I am good at ballet." Children with self-confidence trust in their abilities, have realistic expectations, know their strengths and weaknesses, are able to adjust to difficult situations, and meet different challenges presented to them. When children exhibit self-confidence they tend to jump into novel situations with realistic thoughts about being successful at a task.

Self-confidence is not built overnight; rather, it is built through repeated practice over time. Practicing in small steps builds confidence. Making accurate judgments about how next to improve builds confidence. Persisting even if mistakes are made builds confidence. As children mature, they become more certain about their skills. For example, when learning to play piano, one must first learn the keys and notes, play scales, understand sheet music, and practice until one is comfortable with the notes and keys to play a song. Confidence develops through action.

Conversely, children lacking in self-confidence often rely on the approval of others such as parents, teachers, and coaches in order to feel good about themselves. They may tell themselves that they cannot do something and may avoid or be reluctant to initiate a task. The less confident child may engage in put-down statements or negative self-talk such as "Nobody likes me," or "I can't do anything right," which may result in feelings of anxiety, despair, or depression. Less confident children will often compare themselves to others because they believe they do not measure up to others.

When they feel embarrassment, rejection, failure, or a lack of control, less confident children may be more prone to acting-out behaviors such as temper tantrums, crying fits, and withdrawal from others or tasks. Because self-confidence is connected to performance, it can be easily challenged. For example, children who are confident silent readers may become anxious and less confident when they are asked to read aloud. Children may be afraid to take risks because they fear failure, or looking like a failure in front of others.

Having self-confidence does not necessarily mean that children are confident in all aspects of their lives. Children can feel confident in certain areas of their lives, while feeling less confident in other areas. For example, they may have high self-confidence in their math skills but poor self-confidence in their ability to write a short story.

Building Self-Confidence in Children

Parents and caregivers play an important role in the development of self-confidence in children. When parents accept their children, even when they make mistakes, it provides the groundwork for children to develop positive feelings and beliefs about themselves. When parents do this, it forms the foundation for self-confidence. Below are some strategies you can use to foster self-confidence in your children.

Keep the lines of communication open. Good communication includes being conscious of what you say, as well as listening carefully. When you hear your children put themselves down with statements such as "I'm stupid," or "I'm not good at anything," your initial response may be to counter your child's negative statements with extremely positive statements, such as "Stop thinking silly. You are such a smart boy!" Although you may have the best of intentions, and these replies come from a loving place, these types of statements may close up communication and cause children to feel unheard or misunderstood. Rather than dismissing your child's feelings and jumping to immediately counteract your child's negative self-talk, emphasize your child's strengths and problem-solve with him or her about how to develop weaknesses into strengths. Encourage your child to ask others for help. For example, if your child says, "I got an F on my science test. I'm the dumbest one in the class," you might respond, "Just because you didn't get a good grade doesn't mean you are dumb. I know that you studied for that test. Science can be difficult. If you are having a problem, maybe we can speak with your teacher to get extra help or hire a tutor." It is important that your children understand that although you want them to do well, you will love them no matter what the outcome of their efforts is.

Model self-confidence. Children watch how the adults in their lives handle disappointment, obstacles, and failure. The way that you handle these challenges will influence your child's self-confidence. When you are dealing with a challenging situation in your own life, be careful not to put yourself down or compare yourself to others. Furthermore, by making difficult changes in your own life—for example, seeking a new job or ending an unhealthy relationship—you model self-acceptance and perseverance.

Focus on effort, not results. Rather than focusing on outcomes—an A on a test, winning a game—concentrate on the effort your child put into attaining a goal. For example, you can say something like, "I noticed that you are studying really hard for your test. Good job!" or "I am so proud of all the time you are spending practicing the piano for your recital." By focusing on and praising the steps needed to attain a goal, you help build self-confidence. Achieving results are important, but praising effort encourages children to work hard, do their best, and enjoy what they are doing without thinking that they have to get things right the first time and do them perfectly.

Practice. Helping children prepare for new situations or tasks can go a long way towards boosting their confidence. Learning new subjects and skills can be challenging for the child who tends to give up easily or engage in negative self-talk such as "I'm a loser!" or "I'm stupid." Children lacking in confidence will be afraid of stepping out of their comfort zones and taking risks because it might mean failure. However, the more children can practice, the better their chances for success. Encourage children to move beyond their comfort zone by taking healthy risks, such as trying out for a sport or the school play, signing up for a more challenging class, or introducing themselves to a new person. If your child is struggling with a task, don't be quick to jump in and solve the problem or rescue him or her. Rather, provide encouragement and praise your child's efforts, even when those efforts are small steps. By doing this, you are shaping your child's behavior and building confidence slowly and steadily. Encourage perseverance. Confidence is built by working on difficult tasks and through practice.

Keep anxiety down. Self-confidence can be hindered by anxiety about failing, being humiliated, or not being good enough. Keeping anxiety within limits can help confidence grow. Communicate to children that it's okay to feel a little nervous. Teach them to take deep breaths, and use distraction—for example, by counting by odd or even numbers—when they feel anxious. Encourage them to visualize calm images or picture themselves succeeding in the task.

Discourage negative self-talk and put-down statements. Children lacking in confidence will often engage in self-defeating thinking, use negative self-talk, and put themselves down. This way of thinking will often lead the child to give up, act out, feel anxious, and exhibit low self-confidence. Some children who lack confidence may engage in *black-and-white thinking.* This means that they view a situation or themselves in extremes ("If I'm not perfect then I'm a failure") and are unable to see the gray or complexities of a situation. They may magnify the negative ("I didn't make the touchdown. Now everyone will think I'm the worst football player") or minimize the positive ("Everyone told me they enjoyed my speech on dinosaurs except Brenda. I guess my speech was not that good"). Children with low self-confidence may also *catastrophize,* meaning they anticipate a negative outcome and predict that if that outcome came true, it would be the worse thing to ever happen to them ("I find it hard to talk to kids. I will never have friends"). If your child engages in negative self-talk and put-down statements, you might say something like, "I know you are disappointed, but let's say encouraging things to ourselves like 'don't give up.'" Teach children what they can learn from mistakes. Change "I can't," into "I'll try," or "I'll work harder." This story offers several positive self-talk phrases including, "Give myself a break. Anyone can make a mistake."

Sometimes, despite your efforts to build your child's self-confidence, your child may continue to struggle with low confidence. If you find that your child is displaying low self-confidence and is speaking or behaving in ways that interfere with school, activities, or relationships, it is recommended that you consult with a mental health professional for further assistance.

About the Author

Frank J. Sileo, PhD, is a New Jersey licensed psychologist and the founder and executive director of the Center for Psychological Enhancement in Ridgewood, New Jersey. He received his doctorate from Fordham University in New York City. In his practice, he works with children, adolescents, adults, and families. Since 2010, he has been consistently recognized as one of New Jersey's top kids' doctors. He is the author of four children's books: *Toilet Paper Flowers: A Story for Children about Crohn's Disease, Hold the Cheese Please: A Story for Children about Lactose Intolerance, Bug Bites and Campfires: A Story for Kids about Homesickness,* and *Sally Sore Loser: A Story about Winning and Losing,* which is the Gold Medal recipient of the prestigious Mom's Choice Award. He speaks across the country to children and families. He has been published in psychological journals and is often quoted in magazines, podcasts, webcasts, radio, and television. You can learn more about Dr. Sileo on his website, drfranksileo.com.

About the Illustrator

Sue Cornelison has loved to draw since she was young. Now that she is grown, Sue illustrates in her "Tree Top" art studio in her backyard in rural Iowa. Together with husband, Ross, she raised six children. When she is not drawing and painting, she coaches trampoline and tumbling and feels blessed to be in her element. Past projects include *Sofia's Dream, You're Wearing That to School!?, Ten Turtles on Tuesday,* the award-winning "Howard B. Wigglebottom" series, and the "Bitty Baby" series for American Girl. She works in a variety of mediums, including digital and oil. The illustrations for *Don't Put Yourself Down in Circus Town* were created digitally.

About Magination Press

Magination Press is an imprint of the American Psychological Association, the largest scientific and professional organization representing psychologists in the United States and the largest association of psychologists worldwide.